LOST PROPERTY

Bruce Ingman

Houghton Mifflin Company   Boston 1998

Our day usually begins when we hear Mac, our dog, saying good morning to the postman.

He always leaves in rather a hurry
(some people never learn).

If that doesn't wake us up, BOY, does Dad's singing.

Oooh! Someone has taken
Dad's towel again.
"MAURICE!"

"It wasn't me, Dad, honest."

I can never find two socks that match.

I always end up going to school
with odd socks on.

Mom spends a lot of time gardening.
She grows all kinds of beautiful flowers.

Dad has decided the house is looking a bit shabby and needs smartening up a touch with a brand-new coat of paint.

Every now and then, Mom goes
to check up on her flowers.

Some flowers never seem to grow,
no matter how much they're watered.

Dad just can't understand why
he's run out of paint.

The man in the shop said he'd bought
enough for two houses.

Mom's always knitting. She's making
Dad a pullover for his birthday.

(I hope this one fits.)

Mom's looking for an umbrella because it's pouring down with rain and she has to go to the shops.

I do hope she finds one or
it'll be fish fingers and chips
for dinner AGAIN!

Mac hates going out in the rain. He'd much rather snooze in front of a nice warm fire.

What's Mom up to? She's found her tape
measure but lost her knitting needles.

Dad can't find his dry-cleaning ticket.

He's always losing things, especially the car keys!

I love playing with my toys.

Hang on a minute! I can't find all the
letters to spell out my name – MAURICE.
There are three letters missing.

And I've got an idea
who might have them.

KEEP
OFF
THE
GRASS

macs holiday romance

M
A
C

Now where's Mac's lead?

For my Mum and Dad

Walter Lorraine *wl* Books

Text and illustrations copyright © 1997 by Bruce Ingman

First Houghton Mifflin edition 1998
Originally published in Great Britain in 1997
Published by arrangement with Reed International Books Limited
Michelin House, 81 Fulham Road, London SW3 6RB

Library of Congress Cataloging-in-Publication Data
Ingman, Bruce. 1963-
Lost property / by Bruce Ingman.
p.   cm.
Summary: Maurice and his parents keep losing things around the
house, and Maurice suspects that Mac, the family dog, has something
to do with the disappearances.
ISBN 0-395-88900-6
[1. Lost and found possessions—Fiction. 2. Family life—Fiction.
3. Dogs—Fiction.]   I. Title
PZ7.I525Lo 1998
[E]—dc21   97-20638
                                                            CIP
                                                            AC

Printed in Singapore

10 9 8 7 6 5 4 3 2 1